j30406

jE
VAN   Van Leeuwen, Jean
        Papa and the pioneer

Papa
and the
Pioneer Quilt

Jean Van Leeuwen
pictures by Rebecca Bond

Dial Books for Young Readers

For pioneers like Rachel Bond, who traveled the Oregon Trail in 1853,
with only a kettle and the makings of a quilt —J.V.L.

For the children pioneers of today, with miles and miles to go —R.B.

DIAL BOOKS FOR YOUNG READERS
A division of Penguin Young Readers Group • Published by The Penguin Group
Penguin Group (USA) Inc., 375 Hudson Street, New York, NY 10014, U.S.A.

Penguin Group (Canada), 90 Eglinton Avenue East, Suite 700, Toronto, Ontario, Canada M4P 2Y3
(a division of Pearson Penguin Canada Inc.)
Penguin Books Ltd, 80 Strand, London WC2R 0RL, England
Penguin Ireland, 25 St. Stephen's Green, Dublin 2, Ireland (a division of Penguin Books Ltd)
Penguin Group (Australia), 250 Camberwell Road, Camberwell, Victoria 3124, Australia
(a division of Pearson Australia Group Pty Ltd)
Penguin Books India Pvt Ltd, 11 Community Centre, Panchsheel Park, New Delhi - 110 017, India
Penguin Group (NZ), Cnr Airborne and Rosedale Roads, Albany, Auckland 1310, New Zealand
(a division of Pearson New Zealand Ltd)
Penguin Books (South Africa) (Pty) Ltd, 24 Sturdee Avenue, Rosebank, Johannesburg 2196, South Africa
Penguin Books Ltd, Registered Offices: 80 Strand, London WC2R 0RL, England

Text copyright © 2007 by Jean Van Leeuwen
Pictures copyright © 2007 by Rebecca Bond

Designed by Nancy R. Leo-Kelly • Text set in Truesdell Bold
Manufactured in China on acid-free paper
1 3 5 7 9 10 8 6 5 4 2

Library of Congress Cataloging-in-Publication Data
Van Leeuwen, Jean.
Papa and the pioneer quilt / Jean Van Leeuwen ; pictures by Rebecca Bond.
p.   cm.
Summary: As her family travels by wagon train to Oregon, a young girl
gathers scraps of cloth so that she can make a quilt. Includes historical note.
ISBN 978-0-8037-3028-1
[1. Quilts—Fiction. 2. Overland journeys to the Pacific—Fiction. 3. Frontier and pioneer life—West (U.S.)—Fiction.
4. Oregon National Historic Trail—Fiction. 5. West (U.S.)—Fiction—Fiction.] I. Bond, Rebecca, date, ill. II. Title.
PZ7.V3273Pap 2007   [Fic]—dc22   2005022983

The artwork was created with acrylics on watercolor paper.

My papa has wandering feet.
That's what Mama always says.
Those feet have taken us to a lot of places. From Pennsylvania,
where I was born, to Ohio, where Harrison came along. Then to
Indiana, where Jacob joined the family. And Missouri. Our new
little baby, Susannah, was born there.

And now Papa's feet have us wandering again.
This time way out west to a place called Oregon.

I didn't want to go. I loved our little farm, and my
pet calf Dolly, and Grandma living just down the road.

But Papa said, "I hear tell land out there is the
finest a man could want."

And Mama said, "We have to go, Rebecca.
This is Papa's dream."

So we set out in early spring by wagon train.

Trouble was, my feet looked like they'd be worn out before
we got there. I walked along beside the wagon: ten, twelve,
sometimes fifteen miles a day. My shoes were all scuffed up
before we even got to Kansas.

Sometimes Rachel walked beside me. She was a new bride. She smiled all the time, even though all she had in the world was a copper kettle. One noon when we stopped for dinner, she showed me what was inside.

Little scraps of fabric, that's all. Just old bits of this and that.

"I'm sewing them into a quilt," she told me. "So when Thomas and I get to Oregon, we will start our life with a kettle and a quilt."

I liked that. Turning old bits of this and that into something new. Maybe, I thought, I could make a quilt too.

So I asked Mama.

"That's a wonderful idea," she said. "You collect the scraps and together we will sew the quilt."

Mama gave me a string bag. The first thing I put in it was the handkerchief Grandma gave me when we left. Her tears were still on it.

That handkerchief was the only thing in my quilt bag for a while. Until the day we crossed the river.

Oh, that river water was flowing fast! Papa tried to
hold on to the oxen, but he was pushed under. Next
thing we knew, the river carried him away.
"Papa!" cried Jacob.

Three men pulled him out and laid him onshore.
He lay so still, my heart pounded. Jacob started to cry.

Then Papa opened his eyes and he was all right.

But not his shirt, ripped from top to bottom. Even Mama
couldn't sew it up again. So into my quilt bag it went.

Rachel told me stories about her scraps. "This one is from my daddy's old coat, and this is the bonnet I wore to church, and that is a piece of my mama's apron, and the britches my brother Isaac wore when the dog bit him."

Her eyes filled with tears. "I may not see any of them ever again."

We decided to trade. A piece of my father's blue shirt for a bit of her mama's checked apron. I added it to my quilt bag.

A few weeks later, we were in Nebraska. A new family joined our wagon train. They had seven girls and one of them, Mattie, was near my age.

It was so nice to have a friend! Mattie and I watched the little ones together and looked for prairie dogs and talked about home. One day we found a whole field of bluebells.

"Oh, let's pick some!" said Mattie.

We picked big bunches to decorate the wagons and more for our hair. I placed a crown of buttercups on Susannah's head. She didn't like it.

Mattie walked with me through all of Wyoming, to where the trail split off for California. There we sadly waved good-bye. "Wait!" She came running back, pushing her sunbonnet into my hand. "Keep it for your quilt," she said.

My pesky brother Harrison could never sit still. He'd
fallen out of the wagon three times. The last time was the
worst. The wagon behind us ran right over his foot. Papa
said it wasn't broken, and Mama hugged him close. Then
she saw his britches all in tatters.

"You scamp!" she scolded. "How are we going to keep
you in clothes till we get to Oregon?"

So I got something else for my quilt bag.

At last we reached the mountains. Everyone had to get out of their wagons and walk to lighten the load for the oxen. But the trail was so steep, and the poor oxen were so tired.

Papa coaxed them. He pushed and pulled, but it was no use.

"We need to lighten their
load still more," he said.
    We left a trunk of Mama's
good china beside the trail.
Mama cried.

But we made it over the mountains.

On the way down, we came upon a broken wagon, its contents all strewn about.

"Their oxen must have given out," Papa said sadly. "They'll have to go the rest of the way on foot."

That family could have been us, I thought. I looked at a pretty tablecloth.

"It's all right," said Mama. "No one will be coming back for it."

My quilt bag was starting to fill up.

As I walked, I could feel every stick and stone
beneath my feet, my shoes had worn so thin.
"Will we ever get to Oregon?" I asked Papa.
"Soon," he said.

We trudged on. Up more mountains,

across streams,

down rocky hills.

The nights grew cold.

One morning the wagon covers were dusted with snow.

Two days later, just about noon, I saw something through the trees. Spread out below us in the sunshine was a wide, green, beautiful valley.

"Is that Oregon?" I asked.

"Yes!" said Papa.

Mama hugged me. I saw Rachel smiling wider than ever.
The men threw their hats in the air, and we all shouted for joy.

So, after six months of traveling, we were in
Oregon. One last thing went into my quilt bag: the
dress I wore every day of our journey. It was worn and
torn and mended, but some good scraps were left.

We had a cabin now with forty acres of land. The finest
farmland he'd ever seen, Papa said. We worked hard all day,
but at night Mama and I sewed on my quilt.
Mama said it would tell the story of our long journey.

"The pattern is called Wandering Foot," she said.
I wasn't sure I liked that.
"I don't want Papa's feet to wander anymore," I said.
"Maybe they won't," she said, smiling. "We are almost to
the ocean. We've about run out of country."

Now my quilt is finished. And so far Papa's feet
have stayed put.
I'm hoping really hard we will too.

AUTHOR'S NOTE

The patterns of quilts tell much about the people who made them. In the mid-nineteenth century when the American frontier was being settled by adventurous men and their families, a popular pattern was called "Wandering Foot." It celebrated the idea of striking out on one's own, moving west to conquer the wilderness and build a new country.

Later, however, people began to have second thoughts. Parents didn't like the idea of their children wandering far from home, never to be seen again. Quilt makers came to feel that sleeping under a Wandering Foot quilt would bring bad luck, causing their children to leave them. So they changed the name to "Turkey Tracks."

If you look closely at the pattern, you can imagine four unruly turkeys running in four different directions, much to the farmer's dismay. This pattern is still in use by quilters today.